MERCER MAYER'S
LC + THE CRITTER K

D0828918

THE
BLUE RIBBON
MYSTERY

Written by Erica Farber/J. R. Sansevere
For Capri

A Golden Book • New York

Western Publishing Company, Inc., Racine, Wisconsin 53404

A Mercer Mayer Ltd./J. R. Sansevere Book

Library of Congress Catalog Card Number: 96-75509
ISBN: 0-307-16184-6   A MCMXCVI

LC

VELVET

LITTLE SISTER

TIGER

KOOL BEAR

SLICK RICK

SU SU **GABBY** **TIMOTHY**

GATOR **FLEX** **HENRIETTA**

CHAPTER 1

MOONLIGHTING

The barn was dark. Everyone had gone home for the night. The only sound to be heard came from the horses softly munching on hay . . . and the gentle creaking of the barn sign that swayed in the wind.

The sign was illuminated by the soft light of the moon rising in the evening sky. It read:

BLUE RIBBON FARM

HORSES FOR

SALE • LEASE • LESSONS

Suddenly a figure emerged from the shadows and began to walk down the barn aisle. The figure moved determinedly along the corridor, passing stall after stall without even glancing at the horses.

The figure stopped at a stall in the back of the barn. The brass nameplate on the stall door glinted in the moonlight. It read:

KOSMIC ART
CHAMPION THOROUGHBRED
WINNER OF THE GRAND PRIX

Slowly the stall door creaked open. The figure stepped inside. A majestic black stallion reared up on its hind legs. The horse snorted and whinnied wildly.

With lightning speed a gloved hand slipped a hood over the stallion's head.

On the other side of town, the seven o'clock show at the Critterville Cinema was just ending. LC, Little Sister, and Mr. and Mrs. Critter were the last four people to leave the theater.

"I don't know why we had to watch the credits," complained LC.

"Because the movie isn't over until the credits are done," said Little Sister. "And one day when I'm a famous movie star, my name will be up there, too!"

"Oh, brother," said LC, rolling his eyes.

Mrs. Critter smiled as she took Little Sister's hand.

"That's right, Little Sister," said Mr. Critter. "It's not over till the fat lady sings."

"What fat lady?" asked Little Sister. "What does she sing?"

"Forget it, Little Sister," cut in LC. "It's just one of those grown-up things that doesn't make any sense."

"Oh," said Little Sister.

"Hey, are we gonna get ice cream now?" asked LC. "I could really go for

one of those chocolate dip cones."

"We sure are," said Mr. Critter. "The Critter Cone, here we come!"

After they got their ice cream, the Critters headed home. Mr. Critter stopped at the traffic light in the center of town.

"Why don't we take the long way home?" suggested Mrs. Critter. "It's such a beautiful night."

"Okeydokey," said Mr. Critter, making a left off Main Street and heading toward River Road.

"Look at the moon shining on the water," said Mrs. Critter as they drove slowly along the dark and deserted River Road. The road wound up and down hills, with no streetlights and no cars.

"It's mighty dark on this road," said Mr. Critter, turning on the car's bright lights.

Suddenly a truck with a trailer came zooming around the corner. It was heading right for the Critters' car!

Mr. Critter slammed on the brakes and the car swerved to the side. The truck and trailer just missed colliding with the Critters' car as it sped past.

"Whoa!" said Mr. Critter. He watched the red taillights of the truck and trailer in his rearview mirror as they disappeared off to the left.

"I wonder where that truck was going in such a big hurry," said Mrs. Critter.

"I don't know," said Mr. Critter, "but I think it just turned onto the dirt road leading to Old River Farm. That place has been abandoned for as long as I can remember."

"The trailer was from some place called Blue Ribbon something," said LC. "I saw it on the side."

"Blue Ribbon Farm is where I ride," said Little Sister, taking a bite of her strawberry ice cream cone. "It's the other way."

"Well, maybe I read it wrong," said LC. "Maybe it was Blue something else."

"Speaking of riding," said Mrs. Critter. "Do you have everything ready for the horse show tomorrow, Little Sister?"

"Yep," said Little Sister, as she licked the last of her ice cream cone. "I polished my boots. And I brushed my hat. I just know I'm gonna win a blue ribbon."

"How do you know?" asked LC. "You've never even been in a show before."

"So?" said Little Sister. "I'm still gonna win. Because I'm good."

"LC, I need you to work the video camera at the show," said Mr. Critter.

"Why?" said LC. "I'm busy tomorrow. Me and Tiger and Henrietta and Gator are supposed to play football. We're practicing for the flag football team."

"You can practice after the show," said Mr. Critter.

"But, Dad—" began LC.

"It's Little Sister's first horse show," said Mrs. Critter. "It's a big day."

Little Sister smiled at LC, then stuck out her tongue at him.

LC sighed and rolled his eyes. He didn't care about horses or blue ribbons or horse shows. All he wanted to do was play football.

CHAPTER 2

RIDERS TO THE RING!

"Class One riders to the practice ring!" blared a deep voice over the loudspeaker the next morning. "Class One starts at eight o'clock sharp! Ten minutes to go!"

LC rubbed the sleep out of his eyes. This horse show stuff sure started early.

"LC, give Little Sister a kiss for good luck!" said Mrs. Critter, nudging him over to Little Sister.

Little Sister was about to mount a gray and white pony. She was standing on a white step stool, holding a riding crop in one hand. She was wearing a velvet riding hat, breeches, boots, and gloves.

"Good luck," LC mumbled, kissing the air somewhere by Little Sister's right ear.

"Now give Capri a kiss for luck, too," ordered Little Sister, using the nickname for her horse, Capricorn.

"No way," said LC, backing away from the pony. "I'm not kissing any horse."

"Capri's not a horse," said Little Sister. "She's a pony."

Just then the loudspeaker blared again. "Class One riders to the practice ring."

"I've gotta go," said Little Sister. She grabbed the reins in one hand and mounted smoothly onto the pony's back. Then she walked Capricorn over to the practice ring.

Mr. Critter started taking pictures with his camera. "Are you filming, LC?" he asked.

"She's only practicing," said LC. "I'll start when the show starts."

"Okay," said Mr. Critter. "Are you sure you know how to use the camera?"

"No problem," said LC. "Video cameras are a piece of cake."

"Dude!" a voice called from behind LC.

LC turned around. It was his best friend, Tiger. And right behind Tiger was his other best friend, Gator.

"Am I glad to see you guys," said LC, high-fiving them.

"My mother made me come to see my cousin ride," said Tiger. "And Gator stayed over last night so he had to come, too."

"LC!" called Mrs. Critter. "Your father and I are going over to the ring. Little Sister's event is going to start in a few minutes."

"Okay," called LC.

"Let's get something to eat," said Gator. "I'm starved."

LC, Tiger, and Gator walked over to the food cart. "I'll have an egg and bacon sandwich, please," said Gator.

"Sorry, son," said the vendor. "But she just cleaned me out of bacon. She had five bacon sandwiches in a row." He shook his head and pointed to his left. And there, sitting on the fence, was Henrietta.

"Hey, guys!" mumbled Henrietta. "Great bacon."

"What are you doing here?" asked LC.

"I'm here for the food, of course," answered Henrietta. "Yum-yum!"

LC, Tiger, and Gator each got a bagel and an orange juice.

"Class One is now starting in the main ring!" blared the loudspeaker.

"I gotta go," said LC. He slung the video camera over his shoulder and headed over to the ring, with Tiger, Gator, and Henrietta right behind him.

When they got to the ring, Little Sister was just riding in.

"Hey, there's Tina!" said Tiger, pointing to a little girl with glasses, sitting on a brown pony right behind Little Sister. Tina was their friend Timothy's younger sister.

"And there's Timothy!" said Gator,

pointing to the other side of the ring where Timothy was standing with his parents.

"I guess his parents made him come to see his sister, too," said LC.

"LC, it's time to start filming," said Mr. Critter, who was busy taking pictures.

"Okay," said LC. He put the viewfinder up to his eye and squinted through it.

"I can't see anything," said LC.

"That's probably because you didn't turn the camera on," said a familiar voice.

LC turned around. Gabby, Velvet, and Su Su were standing behind him. Su Su was dressed in a fancy riding outfit with tall black boots.

"Nice outfit," said Henrietta to Su Su.

"I'm in Class Ten," said Su Su, with a smug smile. "That's 'Adult Hunter/Jumper.'"

"Let me show you how to use that camera," said Gabby. LC sighed and handed it over. Gabby could be kind of bossy. She and LC lived next door to each other and had been friends since they were babies.

"Class One to the rails," boomed the loudspeaker. "All walk, please."

"Hey, give me the camera," said LC. "I'm supposed to be filming."

"Just don't forget the red button is the power button," said Gabby.

"Doesn't she look great!" exclaimed Mrs. Critter, her eyes glued to Little Sister.

"Are you getting all this, LC?" asked Mr. Critter, who was busy taking picture after picture with his own camera.

"Uh-huh," mumbled LC, who didn't want to admit that all he seemed able to focus the camera on were the crowd and the barn and the sky. He didn't know why, but he wasn't able to get the riders in the ring into focus at all.

"Tina, heels down and look up!" Su Su called as Tina came riding past them.

Tina pushed down her heels and smiled at Su Su.

"Gotcha!" said LC, as Tina finally came into focus. Now where was Little Sister? he wondered, as he scanned the ring through the viewfinder.

"Riders, now reverse and trot!" the announcer boomed.

LC lowered the camera and watched Little Sister smoothly turn Capricorn around and begin to trot in the opposite direction. He put the camera up to his eye again, but all that came into focus was a strange man wearing a trench coat, hat, and sunglasses, who was standing on the opposite side of the ring.

LC swung the camera around. This time he found himself closing up on the door to the barn office. A woman wearing a fancy dress, high heels, and a big pink hat, was just running out. Weird outfit for a muddy old farm, LC thought to himself as he wildly swung the camera around again.

"Class One to the center of the ring!" the announcer boomed.

"Ooh," said Mrs. Critter. "It's time for the ribbons."

"Little Sister did great," said Su Su in her know-it-all voice. "She picked up the right diagonals, and her heels were down the whole time."

"Isn't this exciting!" exclaimed Mrs. Critter. "And to think we have it all on film."

LC gulped. He didn't know how to tell them that he hadn't quite captured any of it on film.

The horses and riders stood in the ring. Everyone was quiet, waiting for the ribbons to be awarded.

"Who decides who wins?" asked Velvet.

Su Su pointed to a woman sitting at the top of the judge's stand, under a big striped umbrella. She was making notes in a notebook. "She's the judge," explained Su Su.

Just then a teenager walked up to the judge and took a piece of paper from her. The teenager walked across the ring and gave the piece of paper to the announcer.

"And the blue ribbon goes to Number 33," said the announcer—"Little Sister Critter on Capricorn."

"Hooray!" shouted Mr. Critter as Mrs.

Critter and the audience clapped. Tiger and Gator hooted and whistled, while Su Su, Gabby, and Henrietta cheered.

At that moment a man in a red vest ran out of the barn office, wildly waving his arms.

"Who's that?" Gabby asked.

"It's Skip McKay," said Su Su. "He owns Blue Ribbon Farm."

"Help! My office!" yelled Skip McKay. "Someone broke into my office and stole all the ribbons!"

A hush fell over the crowd.

CHAPTER 3

SUSPECT #1

Everyone stared at Skip McKay in shock. Then they all started talking at once.

"Attention!" the announcer called out. "Attention! The horse show will continue as planned. We will present the ribbons later. Now, Class Two to the ring."

"How strange," said Mrs. Critter.

"Indeed," agreed Mr. Critter.

"What's a horse show without ribbons?" asked one woman in a shocked voice. "I've never seen anything like this before."

"Really," agreed her neighbor. "This is a

rated show. It's downright disgraceful."

"Hey, guys," said Gabby. "You know what?"

"What?" asked LC.

"This is a perfect case for the Critter Kids Detective Club," answered Gabby.

"Oh, no," said LC. "We're not getting into that detective stuff again."

"Why not?" said Gabby. "We're here at the scene of the crime. We're experienced sleuths. There's only one responsible thing to do."

"What?" asked Tiger.

"Investigate the crime scene," said Gabby.

LC sighed. Gabby and mysteries usually meant only one thing—trouble with a capital T.

"Don't you think we should leave this to the police?" said LC.

Just then they heard the sound of tires squealing. A red convertible sped out of the parking lot. At the wheel of the car was the woman in the pink hat. LC stared at the hat. It was not an easy hat to forget.

"What's she in such a big rush for?" Henrietta asked.

"Maybe she's late for an appointment," suggested Gator.

"Maybe," said Gabby. "But I don't think so. I'd say she's suspect number one. Darn. I didn't get her license plate number."

"I did," said Timothy, walking up to the

Kids. "It's HOT-1."

"I get it—*hot one*," said Tiger. "Ha-ha!"

"I wonder who she is," said Velvet.

"Her name's Laverne La Roche," said Su Su. "She *thinks* she's a great rider, but let me tell you, she's not. She has six dressage horses that she used to board here."

"Why did she move them?" asked Gabby.

"I don't know," said Su Su. "But she moved them just last week."

LC had never heard of Laverne La Roche, but he was sure he'd seen that hat before.

"Come on, guys," said Gabby. "Let's go to Skip's office and check things out."

"We can't just investigate Skip's office," said LC. "We need a search warrant."

"So we'll ask Skip," said Gabby. "He'll be thrilled that some experienced detectives are already here."

LC sighed as he followed Gabby. He knew there was no stopping Gabby once she got going on a mystery.

CHAPTER 4

SIMPLY CRIMINAL

Gabby led the way to Skip McKay, who was standing in the center of a large crowd of people.

"Why would someone steal the ribbons?" Skip asked sadly. "It's simply criminal. Whoever is responsible knew just how to ruin my show. And those poor kids who won't get their ribbons. It's a terrible day in the horse show community. A terrible day."

"Excuse me, Mr. McKay," said Gabby, reaching out and shaking Skip's hand. "I'm DCI, Detective Chief Inspector, of the

Critter Kids Detective Club. Perhaps you've heard of us. We've solved a number of mysteries in the Critterville area and we'd like to take a look at the crime scene."

"Yeah, sure . . . whatever you want to do," said Skip, brushing her aside.

"See, I told you he'd be happy to have experienced detectives investigate," said Gabby to LC.

LC shook his head as they headed toward Skip's office. Two little kids were trying to put the broken lock back on the office door.

"What are you doing?" Gabby yelled. "This is a crime scene. You're tampering with valuable evidence."

The two kids looked at Gabby and then ran away without saying a word.

Gabby pulled a pair of yellow rubber gloves out of her knapsack. "I just so happen to have my crime gloves with me," said Gabby, slipping them on. "Now follow me and don't touch anything."

Slowly Gabby opened the office door.

"Don't you think we should leave this to the police?" LC repeated, as he followed Gabby inside.

"When the police get here, we'll fill them in on all the clues that we've uncovered," Gabby said.

Gabby walked over to the desk. There was a picture in a gold frame that showed two men standing on either side of a black horse. One of the men was Skip McKay; the other was a stranger, who was holding a gold trophy. A ribbon was hanging on the horse's stall door.

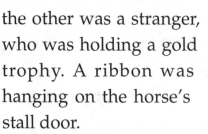

"Who's that man?" asked Gabby, pointing to the stranger in the photo.

"Hugh Holiday," said Su Su. "He and Skip used to be partners. That's Kosmic Art after he won the Grand Prix. He's worth like a million dollars. I think both men owned him, and then Skip bought Hugh out or something."

"Ah," said Gabby. "Suspect number two. Ex-partners are always prime suspects."

"Hey, look at all these cool saddles," said Tiger, pointing to the opposite wall where hats and saddles were hung in an orderly row.

"Yeah," agreed Velvet. "That maroon one is really pretty."

"That saddle is worth like a thousand dollars," said Su Su. "It's one of those handmade ones from England."

"Hey, Gabby," said LC, who was pacing back and forth. "Don't you think we should go?"

"Wait a minute," said Gabby. "Look at this."

Gabby had found a gray metal box that was visible in the half-opened top drawer of the desk. There were some bills sticking out of it.

"There's lots of money in that box," said Gabby. "So why didn't the thief steal it?"

"Maybe the thief wasn't after money," said Velvet.

"Thieves are always after money," said Tiger. "What else *is* there?"

Just then the door to the office opened, and Sergeant Pokey barged in.

"Oh, no! Not you again!" said Sergeant Pokey, frowning at Gabby.

LC sighed. Gabby and Sergeant Pokey had a love-hate relationship. Gabby was convinced the Critterville Police Force desperately needed her assistance while Sergeant Pokey was not at all sure that this was the case.

"I'm glad you're here, Sergeant," said Gabby. "This is a very interesting case."

Sergeant Pokey shook his head. "We're not going through that again. The police will take care of this matter. It's a routine robbery."

"But Sergeant—" began Gabby.

"This is a simple case of breaking and entering," Sergeant Pokey interrupted. "And the police know exactly what to do."

"Come on, Gabby," said LC, pulling Gabby out of the office.

LC and the Kids went to the barn. Suddenly a figure in a hat and a trench coat walked out of a stall ahead of them. But as soon as the person spotted the Critter Kids, he took off and ran outside.

"That was strange," said Henrietta. "Why would somebody run away from us?"

"Maybe he didn't want us to see him," said Velvet.

"Where did he come from?" asked LC.

"Kosmic Art's stall," said Su Su. "Nobody goes in there but Skip. Everyone else is afraid of that horse because he's so wild."

"I'd say the trench coat guy is suspect number three," said Gabby. "And we'd better find out all we can about Kosmic Art. I have a hunch he's got something to do with this mystery, too."

CHAPTER 5

STRANGE LUCK

Later that afternoon, the Critter Kids met at their clubhouse. It was actually a barn that had once been the Critters' garage, but LC and his friends had turned it into their clubhouse.

"Let's make a list of the suspects," said Gabby, walking over to the chalkboard at the back of the room. "Number one is Laverne La Roche."

"Why?" said Su Su. "She may be a bad rider, but that doesn't make her a suspect."

"She's a suspect," insisted Gabby. "You

yourself said she just moved her horses out of Blue Ribbon Farm, so she must have been unhappy about something. Number two is Hugh Holiday."

"Hugh Holiday is a really nice guy," said Su Su. "He didn't do it."

"How do you know that?" said Gabby. "Detectives can't let personal feelings get in the way. And finally, suspect number three is the guy in the trench coat."

"I bet he's the one who did it," said Tiger. "Only somebody weird would wear a raincoat on a sunny day."

"That was one mighty long raincoat," said Gator.

"Or one very short guy," said Henrietta.

"A trench coat means only one thing," said Gabby. "He was obviously traveling incognito."

"What's an incognito?" asked Tiger. "Some kind of Italian sports car?"

"No, it means he's in disguise," said Gabby. "Haven't you ever seen any of those old spy movies? All the suspicious guys wear trench coats like that."

"Actually, the word *incognito* comes from Latin," explained Timothy. "'In' means 'not,' plus 'cognitus' which means 'to be known'—in other words, 'to not be known' or to be in disguise."

The Critter Kids all looked at Timothy. He was the class brain and had once built a radio out of crystals he had grown himself.

"Well, he's definitely a suspect," said Gabby. "And we've got to uncover his true identity."

LC yawned. He was getting bored. He was also getting thirsty. "You guys want some lemonade?" he asked.

Everybody nodded.

"I'll be right back," said LC, walking out of the clubhouse.

As he headed for the kitchen, LC noticed that his parents and Little Sister were watching TV in the living room.

"That's not me," LC heard Little Sister yell. "Where am I? I thought this was supposed to be a video of me. Who cares about some dumb guy in a raincoat?"

LC froze. The guy in the trench coat! He had him on video. And probably all the other suspects, too. LC ran into the living room.

"Hey, can I borrow that tape?" LC asked.

"You can have it," said Little Sister. "You're the worst cameraman ever."

"Now, Little Sister, you don't mean that," said Mrs. Critter. "Your brother tried."

"Thanks," said LC. He grabbed the tape and dashed out of the house.

"Hey, where's the lemonade?" asked Henrietta as soon as LC got back to the clubhouse.

"Forget the lemonade," said LC. "This is way better."

"Whaddya mean?" asked Gabby.

"You'll see," said LC. He shoved the tape into the video machine and pushed the PLAY button.

The Critter Kids watched as the picture on the screen bounced up and down.

"This video is making me seasick," said Henrietta.

The picture finally came into focus, and the Kids watched as a woman in a pink hat ran out of the barn office.

"Ohmygosh!" exclaimed Gabby. "It's Laverne La Roche. What was she doing in Skip McKay's office?"

"I knew I saw that pink hat somewhere," said LC.

"Hey, look!" said Velvet, pointing to the video. "There's the guy in the trench coat."

"What's he doing?" asked Gator.

"Looks like he's picking his nose," said Tiger.

"If only we could see who he is," said Gabby. "But he's too far away to identify."

"I can blow up the image on my computer," said Timothy.

"I still don't understand why anybody would steal the ribbons," said Velvet.

"Beats me," said Tiger. "It's not like they're worth anything."

"Exactly," said Gabby. "And that tells us one very important thing."

"What?" asked LC.

"It's not a simple case of robbery like Sergeant Pokey thinks," answered Gabby. "It was clearly a premeditated act of vandalism. If it were just a robbery, then the thief would have stolen the money in the cash box or those valuable saddles."

"That's right," said Velvet. "So whoever stole the ribbons didn't really want them. The thief was just out to get Skip McKay. And stealing the ribbons was a perfect way to mess up his show."

"Why would anybody want to do that?" asked LC.

"Revenge," suggested Gabby.

"Revenge for what?" asked Henrietta.

"We're not sure yet," said Gabby. "That's what we have to investigate tomorrow. Me and LC will interview Laverne. Tiger and Velvet, you talk to Hugh Holiday. And Henrietta, Gator, and Su Su, you go to the library and find out everything you can about Kosmic Art."

"Count me out," said Su Su. "I have to get my hair cut tomorrow. But I'll tell you one thing. Skip McKay is a man with a lot of enemies. He may be great with horses, but he's terrible with people."

The Critter Kids looked at one another.

CHAPTER 6

HUNG JURY

"This is some spread," said LC to Gabby the next morning. The two were staring at the mansion that stood in front of them.

"I'll say," said Gabby. "Mr. La Roche was some kind of oil tycoon. He died last year. I guess Laverne inherited all the money."

Gabby and LC walked up to the large front door. Gabby rang the bell. A maid in a pink and yellow uniform opened the door.

"We're here to see Mrs. Laverne La Roche," said Gabby. "We have a few questions to ask her about Skip McKay."

The maid disappeared back into the house. A few seconds later, Laverne herself appeared, wearing a long pink dressing gown and high-heeled pink slippers.

"You wanna talk about Skip McKay," said Laverne. "I'll tell you some things about that man ya wouldn't believe."

LC and Gabby shrugged and then followed Laverne into the house.

"Skip was gonna be my fifth," said Laverne, gesturing for LC and Gabby to sit down on a large leather sofa. "But the bum called it off. Do ya believe it?"

"Called what off?" asked LC.

"The wedding," said Laverne. "That jerk broke my heart. Nobody breaks my heart and gets away with it. I mean, I really loved the guy. Just like I loved all my husbands." She pointed to the mantel. On it were gold-framed photos of four men.

"Those are your husbands?" said Gabby, her eyes wide.

"Were," said Laverne. "They all died. Monty died in his sleep. Ray had a heart attack. Vito fell down dead. And Oscar— Mr. La Roche, my latest—just died. Nobody knows how or why. It's like I just loved them all to death."

"What happened with Skip?" asked Gabby.

"Beats me," said Laverne. "One minute he was all lovey-dovey. The next he wanted out of the engagement. I'm still burnin' up about it. And that guy is gonna pay. Nobody, but nobody, does that to Laverne and gets away with it."

LC and Gabby said good-bye to Laverne. Then they walked to Timothy's house. They had all agreed to meet there to see the blown-up picture of the trench coat guy.

"That woman is a regular black widow," said Gabby.

"Whaddya mean?" asked LC.

"A killer," said Gabby. "You know, a husband-killer. Like the black widow spider that kills its mate and eats it."

LC gulped: "Well, she sure is mad at Skip."

"And how!" agreed Gabby. "I'd say suspect number one could very definitely have committed the crime. She had the motive. And the means."

Meanwhile on the other side of town, Tiger and Velvet were at Holiday Acres, Hugh Holiday's farm. They were in the middle of a discussion with Hugh himself. Or rather a monologue. Hugh couldn't seem to stop talking about Skip McKay.

"And another thing," continued Hugh—
"everything that guy touches turns to gold.
He's got the Midas touch. I never should
have sold him my share of Kosmic Art, but
I needed the bucks. I have a little gambling
problem. Had a few debts I had to pay. But
still . . . that Skip McKay, he always
manages to make the big money. And he's
stolen a lot of business away from my
farm. I don't know how he does it. He just
slimes his way around, and everybody falls
for his scam. *Everybody*."

"Uh, thanks for your time, Mr. Holiday,"
said Velvet.

"And then there was the incident at last
summer's show," continued Hugh Holiday.
"And the time he—"

"We've got to go now," interrupted Tiger
as he and Velvet backed away.

But Hugh Holiday just kept right on
talking. He didn't seem to notice that Tiger
and Velvet were no longer listening.

When Tiger and Velvet got to Timothy's place, Timothy was still fixing the picture.

"What happened with Hugh?" asked Gabby.

"He sure hates Skip," said Tiger.

"Yeah," agreed Velvet. "He couldn't say enough bad things about him. I think he did it."

"What about Laverne?" said LC. "She said some pretty bad stuff about Skip, too."

"Yeah," said Gabby. "He broke her heart. Stealing the ribbons was a perfect crime of passion."

"I think I've finally got it," said Timothy at the very same moment that Gator and Henrietta came bursting into the room.

"Look what we found," said Gator, holding up a whole bunch of newspaper clippings. "They're all about Kosmic Art."

"Kosmic lost his last two races," said Henrietta, popping cheese snacks into her mouth. "And Skip fired the jockey, Frankie Frank, 'cuz he said it was all his fault."

"They call Frankie the Itchy Nose Jockey because he always scratches his nose," said Gator. "Isn't that funny?"

"Very interesting," said Timothy, pointing to his computer screen. "Take a look at this."

All the Critter Kids crowded around the computer. There was a picture of the man in the trench coat, holding one hand up to his nose.

"It's Frankie Frank!" said Gator, pointing to a picture of the jockey in one of the newspaper articles.

"I bet Itchy Nose did it," said Henrietta. "He was really upset about getting fired."

"No, I bet it was Hugh," said Velvet.

"No, it was Laverne," said LC.

The Critter Kids began to argue.

"Quiet!" Gabby finally yelled. "Think about this for a minute. All three of our suspects sound equally guilty. They all have a motive to ruin Skip McKay. So there's only one way to find out who, if any of them, really did it."

"How?" asked LC.

"One of us has to go undercover," said Gabby, "and investigate from the inside.

In other words, one of us has to take a riding lesson at Blue Ribbon Farm."

"Who?" asked LC.

"What about you?" suggested Gabby. "Your sister already takes lessons there. So it would be perfectly natural for you to take a lesson there, too."

"Oh, no," said LC.

"Come on," said Gabby. "You've got to do it or we'll never get to the bottom of this mystery."

"I can wire you with a two-way video system so that we can hide in the bushes and see and hear what you're seeing and hearing," said Timothy. "And you can talk to us in case you get into any trouble."

"This is our toughest case yet," said Gabby. "But with your help, LC, I know we'll solve this one. So, will you do it?"

All the Critter Kids stared at LC. He sighed. It looked like he had no choice.

CHAPTER 7

UNDERCOVER

"Okay, kids, walk your horses to the ring," said Skip McKay the next afternoon.

LC sat there. His horse wouldn't move.

"You've got to dig your heels into his side and say 'Walk on,'" said Little Sister. "That's how you get him to go."

"I know that," said LC, as Bunny and Tina and the other girls in the class giggled.

"You look weird in that football helmet with those wires sticking out of your head," said Little Sister.

"You look like a martian," said Tina.

The girls walked their horses into the ring. LC followed. As soon as he got into the ring, his horse came to a sudden halt.

"Keep moving, you in the football helmet," said Skip McKay. "You've got to warm up your horse."

LC nudged his horse with his heels as Little Sister had instructed. The horse wouldn't move. He nudged him a little harder. The horse still wouldn't move. Finally LC kicked him as hard as he could and the horse took off.

"Whoa!" LC screamed as the horse galloped around the ring. LC went flying over the horse's head and landed in a big pile of manure. His helmet flew off his head and ended up on the ground.

"Ha-ha!" laughed Little Sister and the other girls.

"Poor guy," said Gabby as she and the Critter Kids observed LC's predicament on Timothy's computer in the woods behind the barn. They couldn't help laughing.

"Look what the camera's picking up now," said Timothy—"a whole bunch of gasoline canisters behind the bushes on the other side of the barn."

"Why would somebody need all that gasoline?" said Velvet.

"Beats me," said Gator.

"Uh-oh," said Gabby. "There's something fishy going on here."

Back in the ring, LC picked up his helmet. He put it back on, and was more than relieved when the lesson was over.

"So, will you be joining us for a lesson again?" Skip asked LC.

"Tell him you think so," said Gabby through the headset on LC's helmet.

Little Sister and the girls giggled.

"I . . . uh . . . don't know," said LC.

"You did very well for your first time," said Skip McKay. "Now, girls, leave your horses out in the paddock to graze."

LC followed Little Sister and the girls out of the ring.

"That's weird," said Little Sister. "Usually Kosmic stays out in the paddock, and the other horses go back into the stable."

"LC!" LC heard Gabby yell through the headset.

"What was that noise?" asked Tina. "It sounded like it came from your helmet."

"Uh, nothing," said LC.

"LC," repeated Gabby. "You have to go hide in one of the stalls. Something strange is going on."

"Come on, Gabby," said LC, without thinking.

"Who are you talking to?" asked Tina.

"I bet he got horse poop on the brain from when he fell," said Little Sister.

The girls laughed again.

LC sighed. He told Little Sister he'd meet her at home. He waited until everyone had left, and then hid in one of the stalls in the back of the barn. He sat down on a big bale of hay. It was just his luck to get stuck in a smelly horse stall. He moved around, trying to get comfortable, when he suddenly felt something bunched up underneath the hay. He dug through the hay—and there were the missing ribbons from the horse show!

LC's eyes opened wide. What were the ribbons doing in a pile of hay? he wondered.

Meanwhile, Gabby and the Kids had their eyes on the gasoline canisters. After everyone left the barn, they watched Skip McKay walk over to the cans. He picked one up and brought it over to the barn.

"Ohmygosh!" exclaimed Gabby. "It's the old insurance scam. He's going to burn down the barn with Kosmic Art in it to collect the insurance money."

"Oh, no!" exclaimed Su Su.

"LC," said Gabby, "listen to me."

"I found the ribbons," whispered LC.

"Forget the ribbons," said Gabby. "This is a matter of life and death. You've got to get Kosmic Art out of the barn right away."

"No way!" said LC. "That horse is crazy."

"You have to," said Gabby. "The barn is about to be burned down. And it's up to you to rescue that horse."

LC gulped. Things seemed to be going from bad to worse. He crept out of the stall and hurried down the aisle to Kosmic's stall. The prize horse was standing there, calmly eating some oats.

"I thought this horse was wild," said LC.

"He is," said Gabby.

"He doesn't seem very wild," said LC.

"Just get him out of there," said Gabby. "We'll meet you in the field out back."

"Hey, there," said LC as he slowly approached Kosmic. LC carefully mounted the horse. He gently nudged Kosmic with his heels and walked him out of the barn.

"I'm getting pretty good at this," LC said proudly as he crossed over the field to join the Critter Kids. "Kosmic's not so wild."

"That's not Kosmic," said Su Su. "That horse is some kind of crossbreed. He's no

pure-blood racehorse. Basically, he's a mutt."

"Whaddya mean?" said LC. "He was the only horse in the barn."

"So where's Kosmic?" said Henrietta.

"I bet McKay got him out of the way so he could pretend he died in the fire," said Gabby. "That way he could collect all the insurance money. And still have the horse."

"We better call Sergeant Pokey and the fire department," said Timothy, pointing at the barn.

The Critter Kids watched in horror as
Skip McKay poured gasoline around the
back of the barn and then lit a match.
Within seconds the barn went up in flames.

CHAPTER 8

GUILTY
AS CHARGED

The sound of sirens filled the air as a police car and two fire trucks pulled into the parking lot. Skip McKay was standing out front.

"All my horses were out in the field," said Skip to Sergeant Pokey. "Except for Kosmic Art, my racehorse. I was just about to call my insurance agent."

"Not so fast, McKay," said Gabby, as she and the Kids burst out of the bushes. "We've got your horse."

LC led the horse over to Skip and

Sergeant Pokey.

"Poor me," said Skip McKay. "First somebody steals the ribbons from my show. And now this."

"No one's out to ruin you," said Gabby. "It's the old insurance scam. You started this fire. You just wanted to collect the insurance money. And on top of that, you switched horses. Where is Kosmic Art?"

"I don't know what these kids are talking about," said Skip to Sergeant Pokey. "Kosmic was in the barn."

"Then who is this?" asked Sergeant Pokey, pointing to the horse LC was holding.

"I have no idea," said Skip.

"It's all over, McKay," said Gabby. "We've got you on tape, starting the fire."

"That's absurd," said Skip. "Why would I start the fire?"

"Gabby, I told you to stay out of this!" boomed Sergeant Pokey.

"Sergeant, just look at the tape," insisted Gabby. "You know what they say—a picture is worth a thousand words."

Timothy set up the tape and played it on his computer. It showed some scenic views of the barn, but the rest of the tape was completely blank.

"What happened?" asked Gabby.

"I guess we ran out of tape," said Timothy.

"Gabby!" boomed Sergeant Pokey. "That's quite enough."

"I told you these kids didn't know what they were talking about," said Skip McKay. "I could sue for slander."

"I'm telling you, Sergeant, I know McKay moved that horse," said Gabby. "I just know it. He probably did it under the cover of darkness right before the horse show, and then hid him somewhere deserted where no one would ever find him."

Suddenly LC remembered the night when a truck and trailer had almost collided with his car. "We almost got hit the other night by this truck and trailer on River Road," said LC.

"That's because you had on your brights—" began Skip McKay.

All eyes turned to Skip McKay.

"I . . . I mean—" stammered Skip.

"You mean you hid Kosmic Art at Old River Farm," said LC.

"So, it was you, after all, McKay," said Sergeant Pokey. "These kids were right. You burned down the barn so you could collect the insurance money. But first you moved your valuable racehorse out of the way."

"You have no proof of that," said Skip.

"I bet Kosmic is at Old River Farm this very moment," said LC.

"We'll settle this right now," said Sergeant Pokey. He radioed his deputy to check the barn.

The reply soon came. "No horse there," the deputy called back. "But I did see hoofprints leading in and out of the barn. And they looked pretty fresh. Along with some horse, uh, manure that smelled pretty fresh, too."

Suddenly a figure on a big black horse came riding up to them.

"Kosmic is okay," said the rider. "Thank goodness! I was so worried about him. I love this horse more than life."

"Who are you?" asked Sergeant Pokey.

"I'm Frankie Frank," said the man. "I realized Kosmic was missing when I was at the horse show. I've been looking everywhere for him. I finally found him in the abandoned barn at Old River Farm."

"Well, it looks like it's curtains for you, McKay," said Sergeant Pokey, putting handcuffs on Skip McKay.

"I have to call my lawyer," said Skip McKay. "This is ridiculous."

"You did a fine job, Gabby," Sergeant Pokey said with a smile. "Maybe one day you'll be on the force. *Long* after I'm retired." He laughed.

"I could never have done it without my friends," said Gabby. "That's why we're the Critter Kids Detective Club, right?"

"Right!" yelled the Kids.

LC smiled. Maybe they deserved a blue ribbon, too.